A Visit to Santa Claus

Illustrated by Margaret Evans Price

MMX ✶ GREEN TIGER PRESS

I'll tell you a story of Teddy Malleen
And his wonderful trip in a flying machine.

Now Teddy was just an everyday boy,
His Mother's delight and his Father's joy.
Working and playing he spent his days,
At all sorts of things, in all sorts of ways.

And sometimes at night, when he went to bed,
Strange fancies of flying came into his head.
(While his Mother patted and tucked him in)
And then his adventures would really begin.

STRANGE FANCIES OF FLYING CAME INTO HIS HEAD
WHILE HIS MOTHER PATTED AND TUCKED HIM IN

With a chug and a whir the engine would beat,
All dressed snug and warm he would jump to his seat,
And like some great bird his ship could be seen
Sailing away with young Teddy Malleen.

'Twas a beautiful airship–strong and light–
And it sailed the fastest by pale moonlight;
Oh! Many a trip had our Teddy Malleen
In his run-about, flying machine.

On the week before Christmas when Teddy sailed forth,
He steered his ship so it went due North,
And he never once faltered or stopped, because,
He was going to visit old Santa Claus.

HE LANDED WITH EASE ON A CAKE OF ICE

Now Santa Claus lives, as all children know,
In a land that is bounded by ice and snow,
And each snowy hummock and icy dome
Appeared to our Teddy like Santa's home.

So he circled about like a wonderful bird
Until, far below him, he suddenly heard
A sound all good children love to hear.
'Twas the tinkling bells of the eight reindeer.

Then downward he swooped – and so, in a trice
He landed with ease on a cake of ice.

And there, in a house made all of snow,
In eight box stalls which stood in a row,
Were Dasher and Dancer and Prancer and Vixen,
Comet and Cupid and Donner and Blitzen.

With Santa a little behind the scenes
Preparing their supper of Christmas greens.

The reindeer looked up in some surprise,
But Santa Claus smiled, with twinkling eyes.
Said Ted: "I've come in my airship *Pranks*
To bring you a load of Christmas thanks."

Santa Claus laughed as he said: "That's good.
But I wish you had also brought us food.
I can't make my reindeer–by any means
Eat a single thing but Christmas greens."

Then Teddy saw Vixen, with strong white teeth
Greedily crunching a holly wreath
While Comet and Cupid (as one would know)
More daintily munched some mistletoe.

Donner and Blitzen were on their knees
Browsing on tops of hemlock trees.
While Prancer and Dasher and Dancer–three–
Devoured a municipal Christmas tree.

"You see," said Santa, "Before they fly
Those many miles across the sky,
I give them as much as they can eat
To make them strong and sure and fleet."

Said Teddy: "Some boys and girls are keen
To have you come in a flying machine,
'Twould carry you quickly far and near
And save the strength of your eight reindeer."

Then the reindeer snorted and shook each horn,
And Santa Claus spoke with righteous scorn:
"Not a chick nor a child but they call friend—
Would you bring their pleasure to such an end?"

NOT A CHICK NOR A CHILD BUT THEY CALL FRIEND

DO YOU KNOW WHY I GIVE YOU—GIRLS AND BOYS—
SO MANY, MANY BEAUTIFUL TOYS?

"I wish you could see them on Christmas Eve
When my sleigh is packed and ready to leave.
Such dancing and prancing—and then—away!
Would you spoil all their fun on Christmas Day?"

Now hurry, to work! We'll pack the toys
For all of the earth-world girls and boys,
Just carry this drum and train and track
And tuck them inside my canvas pack.

And then in my work shop, we'll fix the last
Of the boats that need a sail or a mast.
The dolls are dressed, and the soldiers packed,
The candy boxed, and the books all stacked.

There's something here for every baby,
And extras, too, for new ones maybe.
It's sometimes really most bewilderin'
For every year there seem to be more children.

And maybe you children can help me out,
(It is something I would like to talk about)
Each year my reindeers' work grows harder
While smaller each year has grown our larder.

WILL YOU TELL ALL CHILDREN, WHEN CHRISTMAS IS O'ER
TO PLACE THEIR GREENS OUTSIDE THE DOOR?

So tell the children, when Christmas is o'er,
To place their greens outside the door
Most gladly we'll come—with pack and sleigh,
And carry them—every one—away.

"It will give us food to last a year
Of course we keep it on ice, up here.
But now, dear Teddy, you must be gone
I see the glow of the coming dawn."

So Teddy patted each friendly deer
And said good-bye with a parting tear.
To Santa he gave a big bear hug
Then cranked his engine with turn and tug.

And back he came gloating and dipping and diving
And wasn't he lucky? For on his arriving
He had scarce got in bed when without any warning
In came his dear Mother to bid him, "Good morning."

GREEN TIGER PRESS

COPYRIGHT © 2010, BLUE LANTERN STUDIO

ISBN 13 978-1-59583-392-1

THIS PRODUCT CONFORMS TO CPSIA 2008

FIRST PRINTING PRINTED IN CHINA ALL RIGHTS RESERVED

THIS IS A REPRINT OF A BOOK FIRST PUBLISHED BY THE STECHER LITHO COMPANY IN 1916

LAUGHING ELEPHANT BOOKS

3645 INTERLAKE AVENUE NORTH **SEATTLE, WA** 98103

LAUGHINGELEPHANT.COM